T0128630

The most beautiful Dinosaur I ever saw

CHARLOTTE VDOVYCHENKO

To order additional copies of this book, contact:
Xlibris
844-714-8691
www.Xlibris.com
Orders@Xlibris.com

ISBN: Softcover   978-1-6698-0060-6
        EBook   978-1-6698-0059-0

Print information available on the last page

Rev. date: 11/24/2021

This book is dedicated to Jesse Li and Eric Su, for being good role models and big brother to Mark my son, at Texas Academy of Math and Science (TAMS). Our family will always remember their kindness and support for Mark, while he learned to live a college life at age 15 on UNT campus. We will forever be greatful to these two noble young men.

I am excited this morning because it is Saturday! YAY! I am even more excited that I get to go to the kid's club!

The kids club is where I get to play at the gym while mom and dad exercise.

While mom and dad go upstairs to do their work out, I get to play with my friends' downstairs.

At the kid's club, I get to play with kids from different schools. We play indoor soccer, basketball, wall climbing, and video games.

I have been coming to the kid's club since I was 3 yrs. old. Before that, I would stay with grandma and grandpa when mom and dad went to the gym to work out.

Now that I am 5yrs old, I feel right at home at the gym. I get to relax and play, and, I know every kid who comes to the kids club too. This makes me feel popular. One day, my dad even joked, that I get more exercise than him, because I ran around the room with my gym friends a lot! teehee....

Wait! Why is my brother Jesse being dropped off with me this morning, why is he not going to grandma and grandpa as always?

Ooooh! Yesterday was his 3rd birthday, which means he gets to start coming to the gym, just like I did, when I turned 3yrs old.

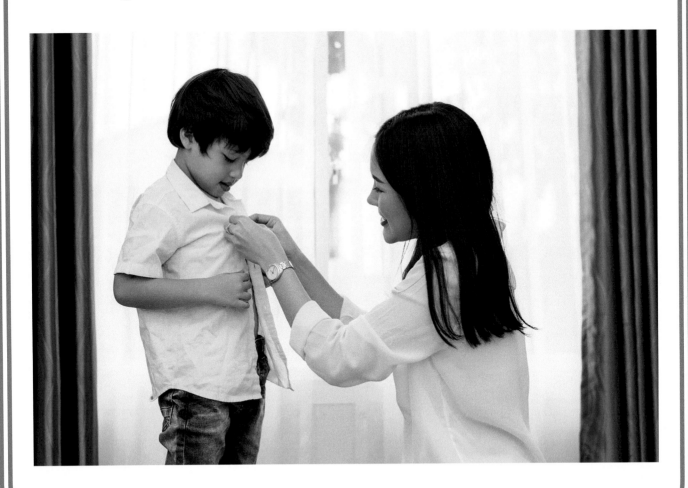

Now this makes me really mad! He will get all the attention, just like he does at home!

Ever since Jesse was born, I feel invisible. It feels like no one notices me anymore. They all talk about how cute my baby brother is.

I feel the only joy I have is gone, with Jesse coming here too!

Well, I am so mad, I think I'm just going to pretend that I don't know him!

Oh no! Here he comes!

Go away Jesse!

Oh no please stop crying....it is too late!

Here comes the kids club attendant.

I hope she did not see me push Jesse.

I pushed him so hard, he fell and yelled out a loud cry. I think he just got me into trouble, and it is only his first day here! It was a bad idea for mom and dad to start dropping him off with me.

Then, the attendant asked me. "Janice, why did you push your brother? Don't you know that he looks up to you, and admires you?" "What does that mean? Looks up to me, and admires me?" I asked. "Well baby brothers think their big sisters are so cool, and they look up to them, to learn from them. You see, you become their first role model!" she replied. "What is a role model", I asked the attendant again. "Well a role model is someone you admire so much, you wish to be just like them, and even copy everything they do!" She explained. I understood I was to be a good big sister to Jesse, so I gave him the keyboard for the computer game I was playing.

Suddenly, the most beautiful Dinosaur I ever saw appeared on the screen!

"Wait!" I said to Jesse, "what did you just do? I mean do it again! Do it again!"

He smiled big, and while giggling, he hit the button again, and another more beautiful drawing of a dinosaur appeared!

Then, I tried hitting the button. A nice drawing of different dinosaurs appeared, just like Jesse's.

I even found out, there were also instructions on how to paint my own Dinosaur, and it felt real!

Then seeing how excited I was about the dinosaurs on my screen, the Kids club attendant told me it is called virtual painting. That is when you paint using brush and paint, except you do it all on the computer screen.

COLORING BOOK

I thought it was the coolest thing to do!

I looked at Jesse, and from that day, I started to admire my younger brother, and he too became my role model!

Printed in the United States
by Baker & Taylor Publisher Services